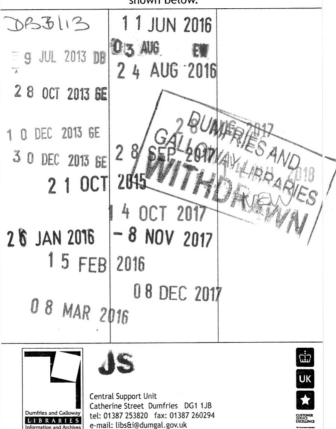

First published in 2009
by Wayland

This paperback edition published in 2010 by Wayland

Text copyright © Andy Blackford 2009
Illustration copyright © Marijke Van Veldhoven 2009

Reprinted in 2012 by Wayland

Wayland
338 Euston Road
London NW1 3BH

Wayland Australia
Level 17/207 Kent Street
Sydney, NSW 2000

The rights of Andy Blackford to be identified as the Author and
Marijke Van Veldhoven to be identified as the Illustrator of this Work have been
asserted by them in accordance with the Copyright, Designs and Patents Act, 1988.

Series Editor: Louise John
Cover design: Paul Cherrill
Design: D.R.ink
Consultant: Shirley Bickler

A CIP catalogue record for this book is available from the British Library.

ISBN 9780750258067 (hbk)
ISBN 9780750259620 (pbk)

Printed in China

Wayland is a division of Hachette Children's Books,
an Hachette UK Company

www.hachette.co.uk

Jack and the Magic Beans

Written by Andy Blackford
Illustrated by Marijke Van Veldhoven

WAYLAND

Jack went to the supermarket
with Mum.

He sat in the trolley and read **Jack and the Beanstalk**.

It was his favourite book
because the boy in the story
was called Jack, too.

Grandma and Grandpa were coming to stay, so Mum bought lots of food.

"I think I'll make bean soup
tonight!" she said.

Mum carried the shopping into the house. Jack carried the beans.

"Oh, no! We forgot to buy strawberries!" said Mum. "And now the shops are shut. What a pity!"

Jack heard a funny noise.
It was coming from the beans.

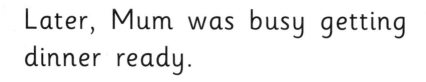

Later, Mum was busy getting
dinner ready.

14

"I don't know what I'm going
to do without the strawberries!"
she said.

"I know what we can do!"
said Jack.

He ran through the kitchen
and into the garden.

"Jack! Where are you going?"
shouted Mum.

"Is anything the matter, dear?" asked Dad.

"First I forgot to buy the strawberries for pudding. And now I can't find the beans for the soup!" said Mum.

Then Jack came in from the garden. He was holding the empty bean packet.

"Don't worry, Mum," he said.
"Everything will be all right!"

Jack's mum was cross.
"What do you mean, Jack?"
she said. "And what have you
done with my beans?"

"They were magic beans, just like the ones in my book. So I went outside and planted them," said Jack.

"Quick! Come and look at this in the garden!" shouted Jack's dad.

Outside the window were five enormous plants. They were as tall as Jack's house. A different kind of fruit was growing on each plant.

There were blackberries,
raspberries, blueberries – and
lots of lovely, juicy strawberries.

The last plant was covered in beans, just like the ones Jack had planted.

"Who told you to plant the beans, Jack?" asked Mum.

"The beans did!" said Jack.
"That's silly. Beans can't
talk!" said Jack's dad.

"Oh, yes they can!" Jack replied. "That's why my book's called **Jack and the Beans Talk!**"

START READING is a series of highly enjoyable books for beginner readers. **The books have been carefully graded to match the Book Bands widely used in schools.** This enables readers to be sure they choose books that match their own reading ability.

Look out for the Band colour on the book in our Start Reading logo.

The Bands are:

Pink Band 1

Red Band 2

Yellow Band 3

Blue Band 4

Green Band 5

Orange Band 6

Turquoise Band 7

Purple Band 8

Gold Band 9

START READING books can be read independently or shared with an adult. They promote the enjoyment of reading through satisfying stories supported by fun illustrations.

Andy Blackford used to play guitar in a rock band. Besides books, he writes about running and scuba diving. He has run across the Sahara Desert and dived with tiger sharks. He lives in the country with his wife and daughter, a friendly collie dog and a grumpy cat.

Marijke Van Veldhoven loves to make people laugh. At school she liked drawing cartoons of her friends and teachers that had everyone in hysterics! She lives happily in the Netherlands with her dog and two cats and enjoys long walks.